CW00408811

I'LL BE BACK – Boris Johnson.
A very short autobiography
An entirely satirical look at the life of the erstwhile PM, a number of other public figures and a range of institutions.

First Printing: 2022
ISBN: 9798352157060

I'LL BE BACK

- Boris Johnson.

A very short autobiography

Geoff Bunn

with illustrations by Cheryl Harding

Younger years

I was born Alexander Boris 'Winston' de Piffle Johnson, on 19th June 1964. And I shall come back to that rather infamous date in a jiffy. But first, a word about the De Piffle part of my name, because folk often ask me about that.

In fact it's quite a funny story, really: a great grandfather of mine owned a fair bit of land. As you can probably imagine. And on that land, he had a few dozen peasant types eking out a pretty raw sort of living. Now their lives were hard. Yes they were. And I'd be the first to admit that. But their penury did help establish the wealth of my own family, which just goes to show that there are silver linings to every cloud. And to celebrate that acquisition of yet more wealth, that same grandfather invented the expression *'de piffle'*.

How? Why? What did it mean? Well, to put it briefly, whenever one of his impoverished tenants came to him, to plead their case in some respect or other, the old fellow simply did not want to speak to them. That wasn't because he was too busy or anything like that, but rather because he regarded the poor as some sort of low-life. So when they tried to engage him in conversation, along the lines of, "Oh dear Lord Johnson, our crops have failed again, I cannot afford to pay my rent. Please may we have more time to blah blah blah" or whatever, his terse reply was invariably "De Piffle".

It was a nonsensical word, of course. But, basically, it meant F... Off.

Then he would set the dogs on the tenant in question and, sometimes, give them both barrels of a shotgun, too.

Great fun!

The even funnier thing was that whenever he told us that story, he would invariably say it though a large mouthful of cake and brandy – the two mixed gummily together – and crumbs would go everywhere as he guffawed the words out.

And so, ever since his time, my family have kept those words, De Piffle, as part of our name. In part to remind us that we are incredibly rich, and in part to give us a chuckle or two at those who are not.

Of course these days we no longer set the dogs on the poor. No, no, we simply tax them far too much and con them left, right and centre. It has the same effect, really. Keeps them in their place. What?

Now, as promised, and with the greatest of respect to the very many good folk who must have been born on that same day, I turn my attention to 19th June 1964. Something of a 'black day' for this great nation of ours.

Here, I know what you are thinking, "Was it a black day because you were born, Boris?"

Well no, that's not what I mean.

For those of you who don't know, June 19th 1964 was the very day that a good number of former African colonies left our protective, sheltering, benign, colonial umbrella. They sailed away from England, or the United Kingdom as some folk misguidedly call it, and went their own jolly way. Countries such as Ghana, Togo, Bongobongoland and lots of other pickaninny places, effectively packed their bags and left us.

Now some of you may wonder why that was such a bad day. After all... those nations were African. And so they were a long way off. And, as we all know, the likes of the Jocks and the Welsh are much closer to home, and they are trouble enough. Well, the fact of it was, that for those countries, their departure meant losing things like warm beer, safari tourists and the like. But for us, or at least for some of us, back here in England, it meant losing ready access to things like diamonds, ivory, oil and gas and other precious mineral reserves.

So yes, I have to admit it, that was my birth date. That sad day. Not the most auspicious of arrivals in this happy globe of ours, eh?

Of course some of what I have just said above, I have to admit, is factually awry. In fact, to be briefly truthful, most of it is. Most of that stuff about Ghana and what have you is total balderdash. Those countries and others went their own way at quite different times. But I have long since discovered that the odd factual blip in life, here and there, however large, doesn't much matter. Nobody really notices, nor do they care, nor can they do anything about it, and nor does it make any difference to what I am trying to say here: namely, that some days are bad days – and others are good days. And that is a pretty deep and rather damned important lesson, if I may say so.

So there you have the stories behind my name, and my date of birth.

Whatever comes next? Ah yes. School. Well, pre-school.

*

We were loaded, as a family. So, as a nipper, I had a nanny or six.

But first, before I tell you a yarn or two about those days... I need to make something clear.

What a lot of people don't realise about me, is that I am not actually British at all. Despite the uncanny similarities in terms of style, political nous, character, intense intellect and unswerving tenacity between myself and that great British statesman, Winston Churchill, I am, in fact, a yank. A New Yorker, no less.

(As an aside, I must here note that Winston not only *failed* to be a New Yorker, but he was also something of a baldy. To be a deeply significant statesman, as I am, you do need a fine head of hair. Just take a look across the pond at that wonderful chap, Donald Trump. He and I are both New Yorkers and we both have great hair. And I think that proves my point).

Anyway. Now if you – as I did – watched Kojak as a kid, you'll have a certain view of New York: you will think that it is a rough old dive, full of grotty looking folk, always deeply mired in crime.

Well that is true. That does, pretty much, sum up the city.

But my family lived in the poshest part of Manhattan. And whenever I did need to go outside, in all honesty, my little size twelves never touched the chewing-gum covered pavements of the Big Apple, not from one month to the next. We rode a lift down from the top floor penthouse apartment, waltzed happily – I nearly said gaily, but that would never do! – across the marble reception hall, and dashed out to the waiting limo.

So yes. I am a New Yorker. And proud of it. Well... perhaps not proud. But I did enjoy that penthouse.

Where was I? Oh yes, at some point, we were all booted out of America. Rotten show. And I found myself back in England and owning fair old sized chunks of it, scattered hither and thither. But, as most honest Englishmen will tell you, a good deal of the country, certainly anything north of

Berkshire, is rather a shithole. So we quickly moved in to London, buying a house somewhere called... Back End, I think it was. And we actually lived in a place there with only 17 servants to look after us. Imagine that? So nobody can tell me that I don't know what it means to struggle!

Sad to report, that gaff in Back End, didn't last very long. And we were soon booted out of the UK, too. It wasn't that the Brits didn't want us... no... wait... yes, it was that. They didn't want us. So then we found ourselves back in the USA again.

To be fair to the Yanks, although loud, and with a somewhat regrettable tendency to violent insanity, they are a very amenable lot when it comes to accepting immigrants. So long as those same immigrants are loaded. Which, of course, we were.

But we were soon booted out of the USA. Again. Not sure why.

And with that done, we all crept back to Blighty once more.

By this time I was around 7 or so years old.

Now in all that time, in all that comin' and goin', I am proud to say that I never learned a single thing. Not one dratted thing. Nothing. Nannies came and went. I ate. Shat. Laughed. Probably kicked an oick or two. And made plans to be King of the World. But those few little things aside, I did nothing. And I can honestly say I am proud of that. But then a nanny arrived in my world who changed my way of looking at things.

Nanny Bob, we named her. And she played rugby.

So impressive was Nanny Bob that I actually began to pay attention to lessons, too. Yes. Even me. Not the easy stuff either, but the tough stuff like spelling my own name and counting up to and even just past 1.

Spiffing stuff, eh?

Another year or two must have passed before we realised that Nanny Bob was actually a chap. Yes, she, or he, dressed like a gal. So although, like all good Nans, she baked a mean spotted dick, underneath the wig and rollers and blue frock there was... well... an altogether different sort of dessert.

At first, because she was such a good old sort, we didn't mind that Nanny Bob was a man. In fact, if anything, it seemed like a 'two for the price of one' sort of thing as, at weekends, she could give us a bit of rugger practice. And, my goodness, she could punt oval balls a helluva long way. Got me well into the game.

Ah! But that was where it all went wrong for poor Nanny Bob.

One weekend, we had some jolly visitors, a posh sort of family, Rowing – that was their surname, not what they did for a living. And their youngest was a little gal, named Jolly Knickers or JK for short.

Well... you can imagine... I suggested to JK that she came out onto the rugger pitch with myself, my siblings and Nanny Bob for a bit of practice. And so we all had a bit of a game. Fumbling balls more often than not, as it was a rather muddy sort of afternoon. Then Nanny Bob took the ball and ran with it. On and on she went, he went, making for the touchline and the only person who could stop her, the only person in the way, was Jolly Knickers.

Now, to her credit, JK did make a fine old tackle. And Nanny Bob was brought crashing down.

The trouble was, Nanny Bob's shorts came crashing down too.

That's the sort of thing that can happen in rugby. Part of the fun, even.

Anyway, JK, expecting to see... well.. girly bits... had an absolute screaming fit. As you can well imagine. And from that day to this, even though she went on to write the odd paperback and had some limited success at doing so, I don't think she ever got over the shock of seeing a chap dressed as a girl.

And that too, of course, was also the end of Nanny Bob.

And from then on, I had to go to a proper school.

But what a rotten sort of show that place was!

*

To my mind, a school should be housed in a nice, dry, warm, safe, clean and fresh building. There should be all the basics a child needs: a swimming pool, a fully stocked mediaeval library, a choice of wines, four teachers to every child, plenty of equipment in the chemistry and physics labs, language learning facilities, regular skiing trips, strict discipline and an educational achievement that is second-to-none.

Well in fact my little school had all of that. But I still hated the place. And, from time to time, as I watched Grange Hill on the old TV set in my dorm of an evening, whilst smoking a fine cigar and supping a glass or five of port, I must admit, I wished that I was attending a rundown shithole like that instead. The japes one could get up to in a classroom where there were fifty of you and only one gown! Cripes, imagine that! And how many days a year did those little swine get off thanks to leaking school roofs or the heating not working or an outbreak of ringworm? We had none of that at my place.

To be honest, looking back, and even though I think many of us felt the same, my envy was really only an adolescent fantasy. In reality, we would certainly have hated such a place. Attending there, the likes of Grange Hill, you must have known that you had no chance. And for the parents too, they must have known that their kids had no chance. Virtually no chance. Not in a country like ours, which is still and rather incredibly, totally based on class and inheritance.

Ah well. Tough titty on them. Leaving aside any thoughts about the riff-raff, next up, for me, came what we liked to call 'big school'. Eton, no less. For that was where I was destined to go.

*

Now a lot of people think of Eton (also the likes of Harrow, Rugby and what have you) as a proper toffee-nosed place, where only super-rich kids go, before they spend a few years dossing around at Oxford or Cambridge, prior to going on to take all the top jobs, all the top salaries and run the country – most of them without the slightest suitable qualification for doing so!

Well, all of that is quite true.

But what a wheeze, eh, for those of us wealthy enough to manage the requisite few terms there?

In my own case, Mater and Pater couldn't wait to see the back of me. And so I was dressed up like a proper count – have I misspelled that word? It doesn't look quite right – and shunted off to full board at Eton.

To be fair, it wasn't just that my parents couldn't stand the sight of me. (Though, often, they couldn't.) The thing you need to realise, with really really really wealthy parents, like mine, is that they have better things to do than bring up their snotty little brats. So we have a Nanny as soon as poss, then we are farmed out to one school after another, where we are kept as far away, for as long as humanly possible, from our parents. That gives the old folk time to go off and exploit a third world nation or become head of an oil giant (which, to be fair, also means exploiting third world nations) or head of an arms manufacturer (ditto), rather than faff about with their kids. All the time, of course. making more millions, for the family.

So that was me. Dressed up like a cartoon character, I was smartly packed off to Eton.

A word or two about Eton: there is a myth that homosexuality is rife at places like Eton. That it is, more or less, compulsory. Coming far ahead of subjects such as French or Mathematics or Physics in the curriculum. The myth goes on to say that is why, once us rich kids leave those expensive schools behind, we often become so hostile towards the LGBTQ community. The myth being that it is quite one thing to spend a few years at school playing the flute, so to speak, for senior boys – but quite another to expect the same sort of practices to be permitted elsewhere in society.

Myths, of course, are just that. Myths. Which is funny old word, when you think about it. A bit like rhythm. Where is the vowel? I have no idea. There must be one hidden in those words somewhere, and my own theory is that the letter 'h' works as the vowel. But tiff tiff, I am digressing.

So, yes, Eton.

It was horrible for the first year or so. Just like Ripping Yarns. You know the one. Where the boys are flogged and kept in potato sacks and, should they try to escape, they are forcibly retrieved by the school leopard. And Eton was exactly like that, too. (Joking of course. We had no leopard).

But as time passes, it all rather settled down. And I can honestly say that in all my years there, I learned more there than most boys would learn in a whole week at some scruffy state school. Which, I always feel, is just one more good reason to keep these outdated and wholly elite establishments up and running.

Ah, now, yes. What may come as a surprise to some of you, reading this, is that all the proper posh schools, like Eton and so on, have fully stocked, fully self-supporting nuclear bunkers. So that, in the event of a nuclear war, the posh lads there – and a few of their masters, or beaks, as we called them – can quickly be taken into a safe place. Why do I mention this? Because a rather amusing incident happened one evening when practicing the weekly nuclear-war drill which I simply must recount: basically, the alarm went off, we were given four minutes to stop whatever we were doing, and take cover in the shelter. Now at that time, my chums and I were trashing a very expensive restaurant in a nearby village. Though, to be clear, I was not doing any of the trashing. No. no. Indeed, I earnestly endeavoured to get my chums to stop doing that naughty sort of stuff. Whatever... whatever... in any case there was no way, that evening, not a chance on Earth, that we could have made it back to the school before the balloon went up, so to speak. What did we do? Ingenious as ever, we decided to barricade ourselves in that restaurant, tables up against the window, doors barred, sloshing white paint everywhere – as advised so to do at that time – and help ourselves to every bottle in the cellar! What a lark! The following morning, once the boys in blue arrived, we were all marched back to school and promptly told not to be so boisterous again. Hee, hee. It was such fun. And ever since, I have often wondered if one should duck into a shelter in the event of a horrifically destructive and utterly pointless nuclear war, or simply nip into the nearest decent resto and get totally smashed?

Great times!

But no account of my Eton days would be complete, however, without giving you an insight into my character.

Every now and then, the beaks thought it was a grand idea to invite the old folk around, for an hour or two, in order to let them know how badly their kids were getting on.

My parents were no exception. They flew in from Dubai and Hong Kong, on a specially chartered plane, and popped along in a limo to have a word, as it were. A word, and a glass or two of sherry.

What, then, was the general opinion of the masters regarding yours truly? Well, it will surprise all of you to hear that they regarded me as complacent, idle and more or less useless.

I know! I know! Doesn't that just go to prove how wrong school reports can be!

*

Oxford came next in my life. Well, what else is there to do? You leave school. Don't fancy starting your highly paid dodge straight away, so you spend a few more years fagging it away at Uni.

And that was exactly what I did.

The town itself is a bit too grim, industrial and dismal for me. Not enough light up there, being so far north. But, having spent some time up there, years earlier, as a nipper, I decided from day one to soldier on and put up with the place for a few years. Be brave, Boo, I told myself.

I had no interest in doing an actual degree, of course. Like my fellow toffs, that was hardly the point in going to University. We all had jolly good jobs to come out to, owning the media, running the BBC, heading things like British Airways or a small country or what have you, so we really didn't need any qualifications.

But all the same, having said that, it is sadly impossible to be a university student and not at least make a pretence of studying some subject or other.

So, and bearing in mind the need for a strong vocational subject in this day and age, something that thoroughly prepares one for the 'cut and thrust' of running a big business, I plumped for Ancient Greek.

Why Greek? Well, a friend of mine, named Tuppy Gazoliters, owned a rather wonderful Greek island – not to mention several shipping companies, which on paper, operated tankers and the like, but which, in practice, shipped armaments around the world. (Not to war-torn places, it should be said. We do have some scruples at the top of society, after all. Rather to places which we *wanted* to become war torn). So, yes, the choice of Greek felt almost obvious, one might say. What could possibly be of more use, when ordering wine in a taverna on Tuppy's island? No more confusing dolmades with a dalmatian for me! Woof woof!

But the degree itself was more or less secondary to being at Oxford and having a jolly good time.

Other kids, from ordinary families, or so I have heard, go to university in an attempt to better their lot in lives. (Presumably, they have not yet realised that the only way they can possibly do that, from such backgrounds, is to make a fortune as a builder and then join the local golf club and Hunt. That way, in several generations' time, they might – *might* – get somewhere. But I digress). Well, good luck to them. For me, for folk like me, as I say, it was all about having a good laugh.

The tougher question I faced was how best to have a life of ease and ribaldry whilst a student?

So, and once settled into my college and with the funds flooding in, I decided to set up a satirical magazine with a few of my old pals from school. You know the kind of thing: in print, you take the rise out of others. And if they don't like it? Too bad!

But, alas, the magazine didn't really work. We had some success setting up the front page of the first edition – which, to my astonishment, only took two terms to do! – but beyond that point we did struggle to think of anything funny to say. In fact, no, I shall not tell a lie on this occasion. We actually struggled to think of anything whatsoever to say, whether funny or otherwise.

So – and certainly not for the first nor the last time in my life – I gave up on an idea, the magazine thing, and sloped off to do something else. Writing is OK, but it does get rather boring. It is simply not boisterous enough. So yes, I gave that nonsense up, and instead I joined the Bullying Club. A latter day version of the 17th Century Hellfire Club. Booze, birds and lots of the aforesaid boister.

I should be frank here. Not any old oick can join the Bullying Club. But nor is it *just* a class based, establishment supporting bunch of toffee nosed tossers. Oh no! Because a fair few of those are not allowed to join the Bullying Club either! You have to pass a range of tests to be allowed in. Being stinking rich and rather offensive is only the very start of your admission process. From that point on, there are various things you must do; a sort of ongoing, gradual initiation, so to speak.

Naturally, I cannot go into the details of that same aforementioned admission process here. Oink, oink. Rather like the Masons, it is all pretty secret stuff. A way of keeping you, the proles, out of power. But I will give you a rough outline... well, a few choice words... teasers almost... and you must just let your imaginations put them together in any way you choose. And, who knows, you may even be right:

midnight, candles, animal husbandry, large sack of birdseed, wallpaper paste, step-ladder and, lastly, a galvanised bucket

And with that, and with a large, well-filled brown envelope arriving too late for me to be awarded a First Class degree, I left Oxford, none the bloody wiser.

Politics and other spaffs

My first grown-up job and, I must say, one for which I was wholly unsuited – as, indeed, I am pretty much wholly unsuited to any grown-up job – was Chief Political thingummyjig for that fantastic newspaper, based in London, erm... that one which has been around for some time now, which is... er... well the name of the paper isn't important. It was a big one. You know the kind of thing. Not a little paper, too small for wiping the old botty after too much fizz and mutton, but one of those ones with big, big sheets of paper. Cod and chips wrapper for ten. That sort of thing. Owned and run, needless to say, by a friend of the family and fellow toff who ran the thing in order to bash the poorest in society and keep them down where they belong. *That* newspaper. Or one of those newspapers, anyway. They are all more or less owned by the same folk, and run for the same purpose. So yes, the name doesn't really matter.

Anyway. Where was I? Ah yes, I was to write about politics for that paper.

Now this position, in itself, came as something of a shock to me. To be honest, I did ask the owner of the newspaper to give me a nice easy number, something senior and well-paid, but which would also allow me to spend most of my time abroad. But politics? Really? Then, as now, I had neither any idea what politics was actually about nor, indeed, any interest in the dreadful stuff either.

But a job is a job. Hey ho! And this one, as mentioned, meant spending a lot of time in Europe, drinking, eating, and meeting foreign folk.

Here, I must mention an oft misunderstood fact about me: I actually like foreigners. I really do. In truth, I generally prefer them to the whiny, weaselly and largely overweight Brit. But, as you will see later, it didn't suit my ambitions for that fact to be generally known so it's not something I have broadcast too far.

So anyway, yes, working overseas in Europe was, for me, quite a jolly opportunity. And, by and large, except for a good number of them not speaking English properly, I had a nice old time over there. Living mainly in Brussels, sometimes in Strasbourg, and scoffing down the old expenses as if there were no tomorrow.

And it was thus that, one day, whilst sitting at a rather pleasant little pavement cafe, or to be accurate slumped after a heavy lunch and close to chucking it all back up again, that I had a meeting which went on to shape the rest of my life. My life thus far, anyway.

Here is that story in full: the sun was out, the andouillette had not yet gone all the way down and yes, as admitted above, I did feel like emptying the can all over the pavement. Too much ouzo. That sort of thing. And I actually believe that I would have done that but for the timely intervention of the chum of an old chum from some public school or other.

Yakob – his real name was Walter, but ever since some upset during his school days which involved a copy of The Beano and one of the older boys taking the role of a *very* dominant Dennis, he had preferred to be called Yakob – was a beastly little horror. A proper little tit. And that much, I am sure, he would not mind my making quite clear. He is, after all, still a beastly little horror and a proper little tit and he makes no attempt whatsoever to disguise that fact as far as I can see. Anyway, this chap, Yakob Pea-Fogg, was on the verge of tears.

I tried to calm him down, telling him to chin-up, square-jaw, stiff-upper-lip, and all of that rot. But it simply didn't work.

So we bought a carafe of Chateau Lafleur (1951 – I had been forced to quaff the last of the 1950 earlier in an attempt to wash down that blasted sausage) and we had a good old chat.

It turned out that Yakob was hugely worried. About money of all things. A topic about which I had certainly never given a moment's thought.

What was the trouble? Well, apparently, the European Union wanted to clamp down, hugely, on tax evasion... tax avoidance... tax dodging... whatever. Take your pick. It all means the same.

"So what?" I asked.

I really could not see his problem.

All of the richest folk, shovel barrowfulls of lolly overseas and hide it at every available opportunity. And they have been doing that since the arrival of Beloved Maggie in 1979. That, after all, is why the country is running out of money, almost on its uppers, and that is why you ordinary folk have to keep on paying more and more, for less and less.

If the EU, with which at that time I had absolutely no issue, wanted to clampdown on that, a tad, then so what? It might even keep a few village libraries open. Most of the loot would be moved to the Bahamas or wherever anyway and the EU would only get their hands on a bit of the stuff.

But no. Yakob was adamant. There was no way – and he was insistent about that *no way* – that anybody, anywhere, would get their hands on as much as a sou of the Pea-Foggs' fortune. That was what he kept telling me, as the wine went down and the night drew on.

"Not one bloody penny", he said. "Why should we give over any of our hard-earned lolls to that lot?"

I yawned at that point. The whole thing was getting far too political for me, and that sort of stuff bored me rigid. And I did not even try to disguise the fact that I was looking at my watch again.

But that was the very moment at which his rather dreary tale became interesting, because he then said that "many others, like me, like my family, lots of them... influentials... all feel the same...".

Well. My ears pricked up.

"Really?" I said.

"Yes", he replied. And he went on to name some of them.

Well. Again, you can imagine. It transpired that all of those rich and powerful folk were getting together to drag Blighty out of the EU, in order to avoid paying a bit more tax.

"Won't that trash the economy?" I asked.

Yakob shrugged. "It might", he admitted. "But who cares? So long as our loot is safe...".

I nodded. That made sense to me.

"So what is the problem?" I asked.

"We've no leader", he whined. "We are the sort of folk, as well you know, who would pick an argument in an empty phone booth. Horrid, self-serving sorts we are. And so we can't agree on a leader".

And that, right there, right then, was where my own deep-seated, reasoned and thoroughly principled ambition to become Prime Minister was born.

The very next day – well, a day or two later, whenever it was I next went into the office – I decided to start writing the most vitriolic guff about the EU that I could possibly invent.

I wrote about bendy bananas, wholly made up. I wrote about the EU forcing people to wear safety helmets when sitting on chairs, the EU fining people for even saying the word 'mile' as opposed to kilometre. I wrote about the EU banning corgis – the Queen's (gawd bless 'er) favourite dogs. I wrote about Bombay Mix being forcibly renamed Mumbai Mix. All sort of guff. Anything and everything. Utter tommy rot. You name it, I made it up.

And so, albeit that I was still a hack at the time, my political career was well and truly born!

*

Mirror... Check hair... No. Can't do a thing with that. Check suit. No, no. Scrap that part. The crumpled look will have to do.

Step forward to my first ever hustings. I am on my way to becoming an MP.

That was how it began. My first appearance on stage, in front of the party faithful, to try to persuade them to accept me as their next MP. I say next MP, while strictly, of course, what I mean is candidate. But in the cranky system we have in England... I mean the UK... it makes no diff who you vote for in around 90% of constituencies. They even say, dress a complete buffoon up in a blue suit, in a Home Counties seat, and he will be elected by the Tory faithful.

Well. I don't if I'd go as far as *that*. But, coincidentally, I had been chosen to represent a safe Home Counties seat. And I always wore a blue suit. And now all I had to do was to go on stage and waffle a while. After me, some old lady would have a go. And then some young chap.

But those two, the other candidates, had nowhere enough bunce to 'afford' the job, and so it fell to me. Of course it did.

And with that, I was the prospective MP (for which, as I said, read 'nailed on cert') for Blue Rinse Suburb, somewhere or other. I forget the name of the place. But then I never spent any time there, so it is hardly important.

A short while later, and a general election popped up. I missed most of the tedium about that, being away on my jollies at the time, but I did come back in time to hear that I had won the vote. And the very next day – or was it a few days later, I don't really recall – I took a limo down to the old Houses of Parliament and became an MP.

Now that was a cracking old wheeze, I can tell you!

It was exactly like going back to school! So many old familiar faces in that place. Chums from Eton, Harrow, Oxford, even Cambridge. The lot. All of us chattering away, wondering how best to get our hands in the till, so to speak.

Some old duffer did come up to me, at one point, and nudge me towards something called my constituents, whatever they were, but I wasn't going to have any truck with that nonsense. I was in Parliament. I was an MP. And it was faces down in the trough and get stuck in.

And get stuck in we all did! I can tell you! Not with giving dosh to boring stuff like schools, the NHS, the climate, or any of that rot. No, no, we got stuck into schemes for making more cash. Loading up the top shelves of big business, as it were. And yes, surely, if some, a few pennies, the odd coin, from those schemes should happen to fall our way too? Pip, pip! Well, of course, we immediately declared those few pence to Parliament or to somebody or other. I forget who.

So, as regards that side of things, being an MP was a good lark. And, for a while, I quite forgot about Yakob and that other nonsense.

But they soon came crawling around. Not just Walter, sorry Yakob, but a veritable army of those nasty folk I mentioned earlier, that sort who could never agree with anybody about anything, and they kept on pestering me to become their sort of spokeschap. You know, on the subject of the EU. Trying to get everyone to sing from the same hymn sheet and hoick us, one way or another, out of Europe.

To be honest, I did find them to be a blasted nuisance. As said, there was lolly to be made in politics and, to my mind anyway, wasting time doing stuff about the EU was... well... exactly that, a waste of time. Who cared? Truth was, nobody did. Apart from those tax-worried folk, and a shower of red-necked farmers in Lincolnshire, there were only some aged C2 types down in Clacton who gave even the tiniest of figs about whether or not we were in the EU. It simply wasn't important.

But the Complainers, as we soon labelled them, kept on and on and on at me, and so, finally, I agree to do my bit to help. I would be leader of their mad scheme, and in exchange I would make damned sure it succeeded.

Ah, but how to stir that pot, so to speak? It still looked, to me, an awful lot of effort for a rather scant reward. So I did, for a while, refrain from getting *too* involved. Simply nodded a happy smile when the Complainers came around telling me they were having an urgent meet up in some pokey room in the Houses of Parliament. I would cheerily reply, "Yes, yes. I'll just finish the bottle of Bolly and be right with you", with as much sincerity as I could muster.

But I never made any of those meeting though. Never one. Indeed, it may surprise some of you to hear that I haven't always been the hard worker you have all come to love so much.

Any road. I made a few bob as I shuffled along. Spaffed most of that up the wall. Then decided that Parliament was a boring sort of thing. Not enough high-jinks to be had. And so I announced my intention to leave what I laughingly called 'my job' as an MP, and become the Mayor of London instead.

*

I was Mayor of London for eight years. I think. Or was it longer? It certainly felt like longer!

What did I do during that time?

Oo, I did all sorts. All sorts. Like. Like er... Like erm... well... I was on TV, quite often. And.... er... I had a brilliant idea for a bridge or a tunnel. I forget which it was now. Either way around , I spaffed an absolute fortune in consultation fees for that idea. Whatever it was. And, as far as I can recall, I did much the same on lots of other similarly half-baked ideas too. Consultants loved me.

how i
like
to ride
the
'Boris
bike'

Then – and even whilst I was still wearing Dick
Whittington's old clobber – Yakob and the Complainers
came calling again.

Now I should say something about turds and flushing here.
But I shan't.

Anyway, by now the Complainers were seriously worried
about the EU and its plans to stop so much tax being

squirrelled away in places like Jersey and where have you. Wet pants worried. That sort of thing.

Oh yes, and they had dug up some awful chap, too. Horrible little attention seeking fellow. Terrible BO. Fartage. That was what we all called him as soon as his back was turned. And rightly so, for the man was full of hot air, wind and gas. Spouted utter tosh, too. But... yes, to be fair... I did see that being Mayor was already a rather dull affair, and that here, through the likes of Yakob and Fartage, there was a way not only back into politics (still dull as dull) but *a way to the very top of the greasy pile* from which the prospects for amusement must surely be second to none.

So. I gave up the boring London stuff and made my way back into the house of commons via yet another general election.

I wonder if they ever built that tunnel. Or bridge. Or whatever it was...

*

After my performance as Mayor, yes, you've guessed it, I got myself another seat in parliament. Became an MP again.

Only this time, I had my eyes on the BIG prize. And the biggest prize in Parliament at that time, was the Prize Lemon himself a.k.a. David Cameron, PM.

Prize lemon? Oh yes! After all, I ask you, put yourself in his position. He was in power and comfortably so. Would you have listened to the Yakob and the Complainers? No. Nor would I. Everybody knew they were the sort of folk who would ask an inch, take a mile, ask another mile, take another ten... and so on. They were the miserable grandad hidden inside all of us. So yes, the chap Cameron was a fool. He should have shown them the door. Them and that crank Fartage (who the BBC loved and showed all the time). But instead of that, the PM promised them all a referendum on EU membership.

Madness. But I can only imagine that he had forgotten my so-called 'journalism' from back in the day, the 'teeny weeny' bias against all things foreign in most of the tabloids and, last but not least, the equally pertinent fact that the great majority of the unwashed British public are thicker than ten short planks!

Needless to say, the reffo was duly held. And Mr Cameron duly lost. And, really, the sap had no choice left but to resign as PM.

For a short while after that, there was a political vacuum. Somebody did replace Cameron. That hapless woman. What was her name? Not Trussy, no, she came later. The other one. Skipping through the daisies. I want to say 'Mother Therese' and I am probably not all that far out in my thinking. Anyway. Yes. Her.

But it was same sort of story, really: on the one hand, pretty obviously, she could have kept Blighty in the Single Market and all that. No fuss. No bother. No need for any silly trade agreements or what have you with Northern Ireland. Just shuffled over to the same space Norway and Switzerland already occupied. That would have totally respected the result of the old reffo.

But no. Oh no. With Yakob, the Complainers, the media and a few others threatening her with the boot, she bent over backwards for the lot of 'em and, if you'll pardon my French, pushed her own head so far up her own backside that she all but suffocated!

And what a sight that was!

(As a passing note, I should perhaps mention here that I took very little part, very, very little part, in the whole Brexit saga. I kept a low profile. You know how it is. And the odd time I did pop the old toupee above the parapet, I really don't think anything I said or did had much of an effect on the outcome of things).

Where was I? Ah yes, so the Maybot was out. Following Cameroon out of the door to Number 10.

But now who on earth could be PM and – and, mark you – satisfy the Complainers etc.?

Who else but me! Of course!

All I needed was the right phrase, to persuade them, to give them final nudge, one last push, that I was truly the best chap for the job.

The right phrase.

Ah! And I found it, too! (Well, I paid a consultancy a huge sum to come up with it, but it is the same difference).

'Vote Boris. Get Brexit done'.

Perfect. They LOVED it. And so, and without even having to fight a General Election, in I jolly well went. Prime Minister Bojo. That was me! A new Winston Churchill, to all intents and purposes.

*

As Prime Minister, my first job was indeed to do something about Brexit.

I had no real idea what that 'something' would be, or even could be, but by that time it didn't matter. Not a jot. Why not? Because the referendum had been held three whole years earlier, and people just wanted something doing, anything, just get something done, one way or the other, anything, they had voted for a mess (and no, I don't mean me, I mean the EU referendum!) and now they wanted that mess sorting out.

Politically, on the one side, we had Catweazle as head of the Labour party. So he, pretty obviously, was going nowhere. Least of all into Number 10. So it was down to me to resolve the thing.

How best do that? Call a General Election.

So that was what I did.

On paper, that election itself was a straightforward choice between 'Getting Brexit done' (our nonsensical slogan) or 'Prolong the pain of doing nothing' (the oppositions official position). But in reality – as I have already intimated – the election was much more about a straightforward choice: 'Do you want Catweazle for Prime Minister or Boris'?

And the resounding answer from the British public was 'Boris'.

So, I won that General Election, dashed once more through the door to Downing Street before people realised the enormous gaff they had made, and then got Brexit done.

Who was it that said you can't fool all of the people all of the time!

*

So Brexit was done. (Before you say anything, I know it wasn't done. We *all* know it wasn't done. Everyone knew it wasn't done. But the proles needed to hear us say that it *was* done, OK?) And I was PM. Only this time, I had actually been voted into office. Amazing.

Entering office as Prime Minister, elected as Prime Minister, is one of the most humbling experiences a chap (or chapess) can have.

But I don't do humble.

And my first thought was that "Hey everybody loves me! I really am something special".

Then it also occurred to me that I was now respected, across the globe, as a serious political heavyweight, sort of bod chap.

Perhaps, I thought, there was nothing between me and my childhood dream of being King of the World?

Only... of course... there was. There was still something in my way: me. Myself. Yours truly.

As the more astute reader may have noticed, I am not the most hardworking of men. Nor, in all circumstances, am I the most honest and upright of men. Integrity is a very distant second in my vocabulary to words like opportunity and lolly. I can be bright-ish, yes, yes I can be. But then so can a candle. It rather depends on how dark the rest of the room is. And politically speaking, with people like Pattie Petal and Gavin 'Woolly' Williamson all around me... it felt rather as if I was living in a very dark room. Who wouldn't look bright, in amongst that shower?

On top of that, to wit, my minor character foibles, I also found myself staring into something of a void: with 'Brexit done', there was nothing much else, certainly not anything serious, to which I needed give any of my time or attention.

Yes, for sure, there was that Covid buggy thing. But I found that rather dull, to be honest. I was hardly going to invent the vaccine myself, nor was I going to travel door-to-door asking folk to roll up their sleeves and take a shot in the arm! And I think we all soon got bored, didn't we, with banging our pots and pans every Thursday night?

True, I did manage to shower some shady PPE contracts around, as politicians are wont to do. But even that was only about signing the odd bit of paper or opening the odd brown envelope. Hardly fun. Hardly boisterous. Not for a lad with my potential!

Then there was that nutter in Russia. Or was he in America? I forget. That blond haired loon, you know. The one with the orange face. Complete political charlatan. Oh, no, wait, was that me? No, no. Russia, yes, that was it. Vladimir Sputnik. That was his name. Invaded another bit of Russia or something.

Now there, for a while, yes, I did think to myself – and memories of the Eton nuclear bunker came back to mind – "Aha! Here is my moment! Churchill-like I shall give speeches about beaches and sweating and toiling and so on". But I couldn't think of a dratted thing to say. And instead of writing glorious speeches, I sat at my desk simply folding one paper-dart after another.

Ah well.

And then, basically, it all went tits up.

Hee hee! Funny really. When I look back at my career, and I reflect on all the half-arsed things that I did and the chaos which ensued – and, quite amazingly, always got away with! – it will never cease to astound me that simply failing to call out some old friend as 'a backgammon player' (which, to be fair, he was) was what really dropped me in queer street. If you'll pardon the expression.

And from that moment on, the knives were out for your truly.

Of course there's nothing unusual in losing a few junior ministers or even the odd senior minister. Resignations do happen in the politics game. They happen all the time. And, personally, I don't feel that having fifty seven of them (57) resign, in the space of a few days, is all that much to make a fuss about.

But there were some sour grapes around, in the media and what have you. And so I was slowly eased out of Downing Street.

Eased until I popped out like a greased piglet.

Now you could say, that I was slung out on my ear.

Or, you could say – as I am certain the history books will indeed say, because a fair few of my friends will be writing them – that I had done my job. That me, and Winnie C, were very much two of a kind. And that, like him, like me, like all great statesmen, it was time for this fellow to move on to bigger and better things.

Well, whichever viewpoint you take, I feel sure that every reader will agree with me: getting rid of Boris Johnson was one thing, but replacing him with Liz Truss?!

*

So there we are.

And what of the future?

Well, my replacement, Thick Lizzy, won't last long. That much you can be sure of. And she will soon be followed into office by somebody or other from the Labour party. In opposition, a succession of Tory looneys and losers will come and go. And then, the party – indeed the country! – will surely see sense and come back for me, and I shall return to power. Triumphant. Possibly even carried aloft on a palanquin like a veritable Caesar.

Until that happy day arrives? Well... I dare say I shall make a few bob waffling on at various places, both here and abroad. Spilling the beans on a few juicy bits of gossip.

Giving the odd top CEO a bit of good advice. Who knows? I may even, possibly, be offered the position as head of NATO, or even the UN... I wouldn't be at all surprised.

Oh, and yes, of course, I shall get some bod to ghost-write my autobiography. That will sell a few millions copies. Fill up the old coffers a bit, eh, what? Cracking stuff. You know, that book might even get turned into a mini-series on the TV. And, naturally, should that happen, there would be need to get some tuppeny-ha'penny actor to play the part of me. Oh no, I could be the star. Me, movie star. Ah, now there's an idea...

Other (longer!) books by Geoff Bunn

A Year in Kronoberg

Like "A Year in Provence" only set in Sweden.

Good fun!

Almost 200 reviews!

https://www.amazon.co.uk/gp/product/1792686234/

Or for something more serious....

Dying in Brighton

The true story of five people who find themselves homeless in Brighton.

https://www.amazon.co.uk/gp/product/1704338506